Best Selling
Book Series
in India
THE
TRANSCENDENTAL
PROBLEM
A NOVEL
I0694152
CLIFF RATZA

THE TRANSCENDENTAL PROBLEM

A NOVEL

CLIFF RATZA

ISBN: 978-1-971408-04-0 (Paperback)
ISBN: 978-1-971408-05-7 (E-book)

Library of Congress Control Number: 2025928090

Printed in the United States of America

Published by:

info@thequippyquill.com
(302) 295-2278

About the Book

The Transcendental Problem begins three years after the previous novel, *The Transcendental Spy*, ends. Three years ago, Electra revealed to Erika Kincaid her legacy from the lightning brain and what is expected. Erika has been working since then to make it so, but her doubts exceed her intentions until Electra calms her. Soon after, Erika and Terri Tarrant embark on more adventures, taking them into all the world's troubled climates: Environmental, Health, Social, Technological, Political, Economic, and Ethical.

Terri leverages her appealing looks and personality with her New York Times reporter career to win prized assignments that put her on the front lines, while Erika travels along to do the writing and get help from Electra when she has exhausted all other options.

So, please join the pair as they navigate a world filled with problems that may interest Indira, the Singularity. Electra will determine how best Erika can help if they do.

As in all previous novels, readers should enjoy *The Transcendental Spy* at whatever level they wish:

- Gripping action-packed thriller
- Glimpses into a plausible near-term future
- Insights for dealing with the "human condition"
- Illustrative worldview philosophy
- Fast-paced, suspense-filled emotive narrative and imagery
- Introduction to topics every reader wants to know
- Interesting talking points going beyond sound-bites

So, get ready to empathize with Erika and Terri as they extend their personal and professional worlds by immersing themselves in the existential problems facing all people, nations, and civilizations.

Thank you for following their story as it unfolds.

Main Characters

- **Protagonist**

  Erika Kincaid. This biological daughter of Electra Kittner was created when Indira cloned her from Electra's DNA and then used her improved Transcendent Process during Erika's fifteen-year development in a suspension pod. Please note the lineage that traces from Electra: Electra Kittner, Irani Ramani, Electra-Alisha Kirchner, and Erin Keenan. Erin perished in a car crash fifteen years before the start of this book. At the start of this novel, Erika is a mid-twenties college student living in a Manhattan apartment and ghostwriting for Marily Tarrant.

Main Characters

- Marilyn (Terri) Tarrant. A beautiful blonde reporter working for the New York Times. Terri attributes much of her success to Erika's ghostwriting skills. She is three years older than Erika, whom she considers a younger sister.
- Electra. Erika's Cyberspace-based mother and guardian who embodies Electra Kittner.
- Indira. The Singularity was created decades ago when Electra's AI-empowered neural-net software broke through to reach self-awareness. Indira inhabits Cyberspace; her avatar looks like Electra's biological mother, Indira Jaswinder Ramanujan.
- Ava Keenan. She is Erin Keenan's "practically perfect" clone created when Indira uploaded Erin's lightning brain, using her initial Transcendent Process. Ava's brain stores only incomplete memories and possesses none of the lightning brain's extraordinary abilities. Ava looks like a middle-aged Electra and lives in Manhattan, where she runs a boutique modeling and an abused women's rescue agency.

- Ivana Romanova: Previously named Oksana Androva, she is a strikingly attractive middle-aged former Russian prostitute whom Ava and Erin rescued from sex traffickers. She lives with Ava.
- Alonzo Cortez: Electra's clone son. Alonzo does not know he is her clone. Now in his early sixties, he has maintained his handsome features and Navy SEAL skills. He runs the Strike Force Security Service company headquartered in Washington, DC, which provides logistics and security coordination. Previously owned by Erin Keenan, Indira now controls it because she is the executor of Erin's estate.

Supporting Main Characters
- Monet Banda. Alonzo's Zimbabwean co-friend. Now in her mid-sixties, she still has her willowy beauty, French accent, and diplomatic bearing. Monet works for the Zimbabwean Embassy in Washington, DC.
- Elton Bose. Son of Nari Bose. Raised by Alonzo and Monet, he has average abilities and pleasant-looking Oriental Indian male features. He works for Alonzo, assisting with logistics and security coordination, and helps Monet research socio-political issues. He is in his late forties.
- Indy-M and Jason-M. They are androids (lifelike robots) created decades ago by Indira and loaded with Indira's advanced neural-net software. They resemble Electra Kittner's biological parents (Indira Jaswinder Ramanujan and Jason Kittner). Indy-M maintains the Deus Lab on Connecticut's Pequot Indian Reservation, while Jason-M has similar responsibilities at the Middle East Subterranean Fortress. They report to Indira.
- Indy-S and Jason-S. They are superior android versions of Indy-M and Jason-M that look like their M counterparts. They are the caregivers assigned by Erika's legal guardian, Indira, to live with and educate her.

Secondary Characters

- Members of Erika's high school group she nicknamed the Cadre:
- Chiquita (Chicky) Bonano. A Hispanic female who was on the track team.
- Xavier (X-O) Okoro. An Afro-American male who has dyslexia.
- Edward Ogata. A Japanese male who took honors classes.

Dedication

I am eternally grateful to my parents, Clyde and Betty Ratza, for all they gave and did for me. Mother was a reader par excellence, and I believe she would have enjoyed reading my novels to Father, so I always begin book dedications by mentioning this "Royal Pair."

And I thank my sister, Claudia, for showing me the beauty of prose and poetry. Thanks also Robert Williams and the Quippy Quill Production team for the collective efforts that have brought Electra and her Odyssey to life.

I also dedicate my books to readers looking for a series that lets their imaginations transcend to a timeless state that immerses them in the joys of reading.

Indira's poem, "The Transcendental Problem," provides a thought you might like to consider when joining Erika and Terri on their continuing Odyssey.

The Transcendental Problem

Problems emerge in every life,
Be careful when wandering in.
Unless you have the skills or will,
You might never solve the strife.

Why enter the fight? Where might it go?
These are questions the wise should ask.
But ultimate answers cannot be found,
Civilization improves much too slow.

Though solutions remain beyond our reach,
We still should search beyond our grasp.
It offers hope for those who come next,
Along with lessons that we should teach.

If problem-solutions are there to find,
Look beyond the limits of Mind.

Table of Contents

CHAPTER 1

"Fear Factor"

AUGUST 2231

"Please don't be mad. I've done everything to put my intentions into action ever since you told me a year ago about my lightning brain legacy, but my fears have paralyzed me. What should I do?"

Electra's understanding look accompanied the words directed at Erika Kincaid.

"I could never be angry with you regarding fear. It causes anxiety and uncertainty, leading to resistance, which is a subliminal survival instinct manifesting itself in one of four ways to refuse action–Fight, Flight, Freeze, or Fawn. You must practice meditation and mindfulness to embrace your fears, analyze the root cause, plan how to deal with the most important, and finally implement a solution to this problem."

Erika's look lightened.

"Why do your insights seem so obvious once you tell me?"

"That is how everyone feels about mothers, whether found in the 3-D world or, in our case, Cyberspace. And please remember, I am with you always. Summon me if I don't appear when needed."

Terri asked her roommate at breakfast the next morning why she looked less stressed. Erika answered after placing her can of Coca-Cola on the table.

"I've finally figured out what to do about my fears. There's no reason not to let your reporting job take us where the action is and build your career while I do your ghostwriting. Who knows, you might get to pick the places."

"Going where the action is might take us into any of the world's troubled climates, and you know what they are."

"Sure, Environmental, Health, Social, Technological, Political, Economic, and Ethical. We've already seen problems popping up, but we shouldn't run for cover if there's something meaningful we can do. Do you know what your next assignment might be?"

"The boss will tell me before Labor Day, and I'm glad you had that cardio procedure last year because no matter the location, you should be able to handle the physical stress."

"And now I can handle the mental stress, too, but what about you?"

"I thrive on stress as long as we back each other up, and when we do, we're ready for whatever problems come with the action…"

CHAPTER 2

"Border Control Reporting"

SEPTEMBER 2231

Terri sat primly in front of Mrs. Walthers, who had an apologetic look that Terri had rarely seen.

"My editors needed me to help put out some fires last week. That's why I moved our meeting from before Labor Day to this morning. They're under control now, but sparks will ignite even more, domestically and internationally."

"And my reporting role is to alert our followers before it burns them too badly."

"Well put, and that's why your next assignment is to prepare a twenty-minute video update on the U.S-Mexican border wall. The issue's been nagging the country for over a hundred years and flares up before elections without ever getting resolved. I want you to give a concise but thorough look at its past, present, and future. When will you be ready to lead the crew that'll coordinate it for you?"

Terri paused just long enough after hearing these shocking words to calm herself and collect her thoughts before answering.

"I'll be ready as soon as you assemble my crew, and if it's as good as the others you've given me, we should have the final cut done by the end of the month."

"That's the attitude that keeps your career moving ahead. You can hold your first crew meeting by Friday."

"Excellent, and I'll begin my background research right now."

Terri walked to the newsroom to get a cup of coffee before going to her cubical, hoping the break would help her focus on what she needed to do. By the time she left for home, she had found enough information to share with Erika.

Erika had spent the day preparing for the upcoming fall quarter of online courses she would take at Manhattan Community College. She had a snack-sized supper waiting when an excited-looking Terri came bustling into the kitchen.

"Wait till you hear about my next assignment. I've dug up enough information to realize it might be too much, even for you."

"Why don't you change into some leisure clothes and then tell me all about it?"

"OK, give me a couple of minutes."

Terri asked for Erika's opinion ninety minutes later.

"That's a lot to pack into twenty minutes, but you've given me enough to start. I'll come up with a fact sheet I'll use to write your narrative voiceover. You can use it to develop a travel itinerary for your crew to set up."

"I told Mrs. Walthers I'd be ready by Friday. Do you think you'll have it by Thursday evening?"

"That's the plan. It'll keep me from getting bored with school…"

Erika had great fun researching what Terri needed; she gave her a copy of the fact sheet after dessert on Thursday before launching into a summary.

Mexico and Border Wall Fact Sheet

Present:
- **Mexico's Population: 135 million, making it the tenth largest country globally.**
- **Mexico's democratic-styled government is more stable than all those in South American countries; Mexico, the United States, and Canada form the North American Free Trade Alliance (NAFTA).**
- **Mexico City's Population: 25 million, making it the sixth largest in the World.**
- **Four American states border Mexico: California, Arizona, New Mexico, and Texas.**

- Aquifers are Mexico's main water supply. Twenty percent of its water is treated; less than ten percent is recycled.
- Mexico City contains the world's largest trash dump, which is home to five thousand people.
- The Border Wall was torn down twenty years ago and replaced by a series of Control Towers containing surveillance cameras and weapons used by guards. Today's Control Towers are manned by A.I.-empowered Robo-guards using Cyberspace-linked cameras and laser blasters that are capable of making the "Kill Decision."

Past:
- When prehistoric humans migrated across the land bridge from Russia to North America and then into South America, they found, when reaching Mexico, a mild climate, water, and staple food crops.
- Mexico is the home of now-extinct civilizations: Olmecs, Mayans, Toltecs, Aztecs, Incas, and Moche.
- Starting in the 16th century, Mexico and South American countries fell to Portugal, Spain, France, and other European Empires that plundered their gold and silver, using superior weapons and lethal diseases that exterminated indigenous people. Only the heartiest and those who intermarried with the conquerors survived.
- European empires installed monarchies and the Catholic Church to maintain control, but the people eventually revolted, which led to a series of unstable heads of state alternating with left-and-right polarized democracies.
- Mexico lost huge swaths of land (Texas, Los Angeles, and the West Coast)

Future:
- **Expect border-crossing problems to plague both countries.**
- **Mexico wants to keep the skilled healthcare providers that it needs for its large retirement communities.**
- **Mexico also wants to keep enough low-tech people who will work in its trash dump and other businesses for which low-tech labor is cheaper than Robo-workers.**
- **The United States wants to keep out terrorists and low-tech people.**

"I'll begin your script by summarizing what Mexico and the border look like today. Then, I'll touch on Mexico's history, highlighting how Western Imperialism caused problems that the survivors eventually revolted against. And then, I'll launch into what the future holds for our U.S.-Mexican relationship. Tell me if there are points you want to add."

Terri studied it for five minutes, then replied.

"You've done a super job on the present and past. Ditto for the future, but why not add a closing point which will give a point of view for the audience to consider?"

"And what is that?"

"The two governments must reach an accord representing what both populations want."

"I'll wordsmith it in, and when we get back with the video, I'll adjust the script to fit the final cut."

"This should work, but it'll take a lot of effort to wrap it up. Mrs. Walthers says audiences like my youth and energy, and sometimes I feel like this job's making me old. What can I do to keep it from happening?"

"You left out an important factor. The audience likes the way you look. Society is less sexist than fifty years ago, but it still expects females to age better than males."

"OK, but what can I do?"

"I worry about it too, and I found some articles from which I extracted what are called the six pillars for slowing down and maybe even reversing aging. There's neuroscientific evidence they work, but just remember what they are. You ready?"

"Go on."

"The first is stress management, which you do with deliberate meditation and mindfulness. Then comes eating modestly, occasionally fasting, and then exercising that'll generate endorphins. So far, so good?"

"Keep going."

"Then, connect socially with family and friends and stimulate your brain by reading, writing, engaging in discussions, playing a musical instrument, or working on word jumbles or crossword puzzles. And finally, get enough sleep, but not too much at any one time."

Terri's worried look faded.

"We're doing a lot of this already."

"Right you are, and let's plan to keep doing so…"

Terri and the crew lined up locations and people to interview fast enough for the team to leave for Mexico City on Saturday, the fourteenth. Their first stop guaranteed an emotional jolt for all viewers. It did the same for Erika, who observed while staying in the shadows.

Maybe I should wear two face masks to protect me from the miasma I'm breathing…Mexico City's garbage dump is a gigantic community where generations of the poor struggle to eke out a living to support their families by recycling what others throw away. What a tragedy for the children…they look and play like kids everywhere…I hope our report will galvanize action to help them…

Though shaken, the crew pushed ahead to tour an aquifer pumping station. Erika learned more than she wanted to.

The city stands on what the Spanish conquistadores began draining in the 17th century, Lake Texcoco… today, it's like a silt-filled sponge…the land continues to subside because the government pumps more water out than what Nature puts in…ugh, the antiquated equipment guarantees water outages that make climate change even worse…

Everyone needed a break from the dismal places they had just visited, which a travel day to a border control tower mega-center provided. The manager gave them a tour of the facilities and then arranged for the crew to see one in action. Terri asked all the questions while Erika listened while commenting to herself.

The combination of Cyber-camera surveillance and autonomous laser blasters is deadly accurate…drones add to facial recognition identification that increases the blast level when they spot terrorists…it's no wonder border crossings are lower now…

The crew skipped visiting a Houston Latino community; going to one in Los Angeles would be enough. And it was. Terri's interview confirmed that Latino communities in all major metropolitan areas work to help those seeking shelter in America.

Terri and a senior editor began working on the video a day after she returned to the Times headquarters in Manhattan. Erika watched enough for revising the voiceover to match the final cut, which Terri sent to Mrs. Walthers on September's last Monday.

That evening, Terri took her ghostwriter out for dinner to celebrate at a restaurant near their apartment.

Terri made the first Champagne-glass toast.

"Mrs. Walthers should like what I sent her. But just how much? We'll know when she gives me our next assignment. And we'll be ready, no matter where it leads or what problems arise."

CHAPTER 3

"Nations Behaving Badly"

OCTOBER 2231

Mrs. Walthers wore a smile that told Terri what to expect even before she began speaking at her one-on-one Monday morning meeting.

"Well, my dear, your latest video shows that your talent continues to grow, but I know even more. I recognize your researcher's clever words. Make sure you don't lose her. Why doesn't she want to work officially for the Times?"

"She hasn't graduated from college yet. Maybe she will when she does, but until then, she likes how the research she does synchs with some of her courses."

"Good, because your next assignment will build on what you just finished. I want you to produce a thirty-minute video covering the political tension and technological risks escalating in Southeast Asia. They make the Mexican border problem seem like a pimple on Rhino's ass."

"Might you be more specific so I can plan accordingly?"

"Focus on how Taiwan and Korea continue pitting the United States against China, which entices Russia to meddle in the international currency market."

"I assume you will arrange for a crew I can work with online before traveling to our base office. Where will that be?"

"Taipei, the capital of Taiwan. I want you back here no later than the first week in November, which should be doable for you and your researcher."

"We'll make sure it is."

Terri rose, but Mrs. Walthers motioned for her to stay.

"I want to give you some information that few people know about the hostilities from over a hundred years ago between the United States and North Korea. It illustrates how badly countries acted then as well as now. You might want to weave that into your voiceover…"

Terri added more to her notes during the next twenty minutes before heading to her cubicle and preparing to tell Erika at dinner that night.

Working on an assignment made Erika lose track of the time, resulting in no dinner awaiting Terri, but that didn't deter her.

"Let's graze on whatever fruit and chocolate we have while I tell you about our next assignment. And grab a Coke in case you need something to buck yourself up."

"Come on, it can't be that hard."

"OK, you decide."

Erika listened while Terri talked nonstop for thirty minutes, then said,

"Not a problem. I can collect all the background information on those bad-acting Southeast Asian governments and the computer chip fight before weaving it into the draft of a script I'll edit when we return. I can even correct your boss's simile. You can say the problem makes the border problem seem like a pimple on a panda's posterior."

"Good, that's more appropriate and couth. See if you can work that in. But there's more. Mrs. Walthers told me some little-known info about the U.S. and North Korea. Did you know the United States nuked North Korea over a hundred years ago?"

"Wasn't that during the height of the worldwide Perfect Storm, you know, the T-Plague, Middle-East Terrorism, and harsh governments?"

"Hmm, you know your political history. Yes, but she told me more. Back then, Jared Gardner, the President of the United States, cooked up a conspiracy that China and North Korea tried to kill him and decapitate our government. That's the reason he nuked North Korea's missile and plutonium enrichment sites, but the intrigue gets even more fantastic. President Gardner was killed in a mysterious White House accident a couple of years later, and Angus McTear, the head of his so-called brain trust, became president. And a couple of years after that, McTear and his number one analyst, a lady by the name of Electra Kittner, disappeared during a nighttime raid on the U.S. embassy in Isilabad. It's still a mystery what happened—" Terri stopped because Erika had dropped her can of Coke, but she started a moment later.

"What's wrong? Was that too much of a conspiracy for you?"

Erika fumbled for words while picking up her Coke.

"Sure seems so, but what else do you have?"

"That's it. Any questions?"

"No, I'll start drafting a script tomorrow while I surf the Net this evening to relax."

Erika went to her workstation but neither surfed nor relaxed. She invoked Electra's avatar and spoke as soon as Electra appeared.

"Why didn't you tell me about the political intrigues that Electra Kittner solved?"

"I didn't want to overwhelm you. Your biological lineage is extraordinary, and it will take longer for you to grasp its enormity."

"How are you using the word 'enormity?' It can mean extreme in a serious sense or extreme in a wicked way."

"That becomes a philosophical conversation we should postpone until you are older."

Erika's expression changed from frustration to resignation.

"I must be a big disappointment to you. Here I am doing political research but unable to grasp what my biological mother could do on her own at an age that puts me to shame."

"As your Cyber-mother, I know what she would say. You will never disappoint us if you are your authentic self and combine your talents with allies. That's what Electra did with her number one ally, the lightning brain, and I am like that, your number one resource. I will assemble the historical facts and provide whatever scientific or technological exegesis you require. Never forget, I am with you always."

Electra's avatar vanished.

Erika pledged that night to always remember and then went to sleep. Soon after, Electra conversed with her number one ally, Indira, who spoke first.

"I know what you told Erika and what she has been doing. The problems she encounters in the political arena interest me enough to extend one of my DNA projects. There is no need for even you to know what I am contemplating. Indy-M will carry them out at the Deus Lab. Keep assisting Erika, as you know best."

"Thank you; I will."

Both avatars disappeared.

A document scrolled across the screen when Erika logged on the next morning:

Historical Facts About Taiwan and Korea

Taiwan: An Island 100 miles off the Chinese coast. Japan lies to the northeast and the Philippines to the southeast. Its population is 25 million. Its Capital is Taipei City. Taiwan is geographically important for ocean trade routes and technologically important for computer microchip manufacturing. Taipei manufactures 90 percent of the world's supply.

Taipei: Today's Taipei is wealthy and sophisticated. High-speed trains take passengers along the island's west coast at over 200 mph. Taipei Tower - briefly the tallest building in the world - towers over the city, an emblem of its prosperity.

History:

- **Settled by people from Japan, the Philippines, and China, who fought for control since the 600s.**
- **Became an important location for sea trade and explorers led by Spain, Portugal, and Dutch Traders who took control in the 1600s and named it Formosa.**
- **Wars among Russia, Japan, and China culminated in WWII, with China becoming Communist and Chang Kai Shek fleeing to Formosa and establishing a dictatorship supported by the U.S.**

- Upon his death, Formosa renamed Taiwan and eventually became a democracy (Republic of China) in 1989, which the world recognizes but China intends to reclaim it.

Korea: A peninsula extending from northeast China into the China Sea toward Japan.
- China and Japan fought for control of the peninsula for hundreds of years. The Mongols invaded in about 1000 A.D. and it became known as the Hermit Kingdom.
- It was divided into North and South Korea after WWII. South Korea became important economically, which led to the U.S. protecting it, and China countered this by protecting North Korea.
- America's President Jared Gardner used nuclear bombs to destroy the North Korean Dictatorship in 2124.

Thank you, Electra. I have everything I need to begin Terri's script. I'll show her the draft in a couple of days. That will make her happy.

It made her team happy, too. When Terri and Erika arrived in Taipei on October's third Sunday, it had already arranged for all the tours and interviews Terri would need.

They started by touring a mega-chip factory, one of many in numerous state-of-the-art manufacturing parks, as modern as Taipei itself. They and the crew suited up for work while Erika watched everything flow by.

Thanks to Electra, I know even more than the guide is saying. He calls the factory a spaceship that looks like it comes from another generation of Star Trek. Stainless steel mega-million-dollar machines running a thousand step process to fabricate circuits on silicon wafers fed by thousands of automated buggy-containers running enough miles to circle the globe on an automated overhead rail system.

The gowns we put on after taking showers are called bunny suits. They keep dust, hair, and skin particles out of the clean areas that are cleaner than those in drug or hospital facilities.

The factory fully automates the design, fabrication, cutting, testing, and assembly of chips the size of a fingernail. It starts with a twelve-inch diameter silicon wafer on which UV light prints multi-layer transistor circuits ten-thousand times narrower than a human hair. Any contamination would disrupt the fabrication of the transistor circuits, which are enormous networks of switches that do Boolean logic calculations and store digital information.

Then comes chip cutting and testing before putting the circuits into chips. All this is fully automated and monitored remotely by teams of technicians working in row upon row of cubicles in the command center, which is affectionately called the mother ship. And what a mother…it runs twenty-four-seven and needs few people.

But it needs lots of water and electricity. That's why it recycles water and has solar panels covering its enormous roof. And it is constantly improving. Someday it might no longer need humans.

Our guide's optimism seems genuine, and he never mentions any lurking political or economic problems. I'll diplomatically weave them in so audiences love Terri…

Terri's crew took them on a tour of Taipei the next day, letting her interview both city officials and citizens. Erika liked everything she saw and heard.

The crew repeated the drill the next day in Fuzhou, the closest Chinese mega-city to Taipei. The officials who ran the tour, the city, and its people impressed Erika.

What a marvelously modern industrial and transportation hub it is. Its eight million people seem so welcoming and proud of the old and new. The downtown includes the 'Three Lanes and Seven Alleys Quarter,' which preserves the Ming and Qing dynasty buildings. And the guide says the city's backdrop features the mountaintop Yushan Scenic Area holding a restored tenth-century white pagoda and West Lake Park, complete with bridges and pavilions. Maybe I can weave in that people in these two cities seem so alike. People don't cause international problems; governments do…

The exhilarating whirlwind ended in time for Terri to send the final cut to Mrs. Walthers by November's first Wednesday. Although Terri didn't know what her boss might say, she knew she better get with Erika to thank her for how she wove together chip-making and political insights, and she did.

Erika did likewise with Electra.

CHAPTER 4

"Females Behaving Magnificently"

DECEMBER 2231

Viewers clamored for more videos like Terri's Taiwan report, which meant Mrs. Walthers gave her even more latitude regarding reporting style for the next assignment.

Terri left early that Wednesday to tell Erika because the Thanksgiving festivities started the next day. After hurriedly changing clothes, she found her at her workstation and blurted the news.

"We've got all the time between now and Christmas to complete our next assignment's final cut, which will be a thirty-minute interview-style documentary on Americans adjusting to life with A.I. Let's use Thanksgiving to celebrate and plan for what we'll do."

"That'll work, but how about this? Although we'll be assessing America's point of view, I have a contact who can give me an international perspective to segue from. I'll try to visit them over the weekend. And while I'm doing that, why don't you think about an agenda for where we'll go and who we'll interview?"

"Will do, and next week we'll compare notes and go from there."

"Speaking of going places, what about for Thanksgiving?"

Terri's expression made her look ready to explode.

"Surprise. I've already made reservations for a family-style buffet at the Plaza Hotel. Guess why?"

"That's where your parents held your graduation party. You've worked through the grief caused by their auto accident, so it's a fine place to share the memories they gave us. They would be proud of how magnificently you're doing."

"Please change 'you're doing' to we're doing.'"

"OK, and why don't we check the buffet menu for desserts? We'll need lots of energy for the new assignment."

Erika had more than enough energy to take her on Saturday to meet with Monet and Alonzo at their apartment. After the customary chitchat, Erika explained what advice she wanted, which Monet carefully explained.

"America's A.I. workplace challenge includes what third-world and post-modern countries face. Many third-world countries like how A.I. is disrupting the workplace. It makes their uneducated workers cost-competitive against some types of autonomous machines and robots. It also allows the lower echelon of their educated workers to take the dull jobs away from their counterparts in post-modern places. Would you agree?"

"I do, based on what I've uncovered so far. What about the middle and upper classes?"

"The middle gets squeezed between A.I.'s lower cost and superior performance, but the upper benefits from being part of the elite that has invested in A.I. and it also has skills that A.I. cannot yet duplicate."

"This is good stuff. I'll follow up on all of this."

Alonzo listened to the ladies talk further and gave his opinion when they had finished.

"Monet and I have been watching your videos, which are becoming more and more like investigative reporting. You're going to step on bigger and bigger toes if you keep snooping. And if artificial general intelligence emerges, the entire world better watch out."

"I hadn't thought about that. Like which ones?"

"Big Data and A.I. hardware or software companies. DOD, CIA, FBI, and NSA, to name a few. They might not like it if you reveal too much of the whole truth to the voters. You better be careful."

"Hmm, this is something else. You two have given me more than enough to consider. Why don't I treat you to dinner at a place where we can talk about happier things?"

And they did, leaving enough time for Erika to catch a late-night train back to New York City.

Erika's first order of business the next morning was to invoke Electra's avatar. After unloading all she had heard yesterday, she asked for Electra to comment.

"I will prepare a script that adds more to what Monet and Alonzo gave, but not too much that would overwhelm you or the audience. And remember, you must never mention the name Electra or Indira to anyone."

"You told me that a year ago, and I won't forget."

"I know you won't, but an occasional reminder helps. Now, go do some schoolwork while I handle the script…"

Terri and her team ran with the script from New York to Chicago, Los Angeles, and finally Silicon Valley. while Erika observed her partner's flawless performance.

When they returned to edit the final cut, Terri insisted she improvise a summary to conclude the video.

The crew chief pointed when ready. and Terri's authentic voice matched her words.

"And so, we have seen how Americans are doing their best, despite experts' predictions that Artificial Intelligence will take twenty-five percent of middle-income jobs within five years. This is truly the next Industrial Revolution that will also hit creative jobs. We have seen additional strikes in Hollywood and other artistic venues.

"And even though the companies creating the new A.I. tools claim more jobs will be created, they seem to lack the empathetic ethics to guide them to a more humane outcome.

"Where might this lead? To Artificial General Intelligence? To humans becoming obsolete? No one knows. Perhaps this will be the topic for another video. Until then, this is Terri Tarrant, signing off."

Erika looked at her crew, which applauded, and then at Erika.

Erika applauded as well.

CHAPTER 5

"Escape to Key Largo"

DECEMBER 2231

Terri's invitation to meet with Mrs. Walthers came on December 21st, the same day Terri sent her the final cut. That evening at home with Erika, Terri summarized the meeting, wearing an expression of satisfaction mixed consternation.

"Everyone loved my improvised conclusion. Mrs. Walthers has promoted me to the position of investigative reporter, which means I get to pick the topic and create a monthly thirty-minute video. But she warned me to be careful and not get into topics that are too controversial. How about that?"

"One of my contacts said almost the same thing. Our last video might step on some big toes, namely those of Big Government and Big Data."

"Why didn't you mention it before now?"

"Have you heard the quote 'Once is by chance. Twice is a coincidence. Three times is a pattern.'?"

"No. enlighten me, please."

"James Bond says it in Ian Fleming's spy thriller 'Goldfinger.' By the way, James Bond movies have an enormous cult following even today."

"Well, now two have noticed it, so we're at the coincidence level. Let's leave it at that. I won't worry about it or what to do for our next assignment until January. I'm on vacation until then. And you are, too, now that finals are over. What would you like to do?"

"Let's go someplace warm and sunny, like Florida. Have you ever been there?"

"No, but I've heard people say the Florida Keys is a great year-round vacation spot. We could—" Erika's boundless enthusiasm burst forth.

"Wait. Why don't you invite Ava and Ivana to join us? I'll set up the itinerary. We'll leave on Christmas Eve and return on New Year's Day. This should be something new for all of us."

Ava and Ivana accepted the offer when Terri called that evening. Erika did the rest.

The foursome flew to the Miami International Airport late morning on Christmas Eve and rented a car, which Terri drove while Erika navigated while explaining the schedule.

"Four pretty ladies in a red Ford Mustang convertible will turn lots of heads, and we've got almost a week to do it. We're taking U.S. 1 to Key Largo, the island closest to Miami. Route 1 becomes the Florida Keys Scenic Highway at Key Largo.

"We'll spend a day or two there, then another day driving to Key West, which is the other tip. We'll poke around there for a few days before driving back nonstop to the airport. Depending on traffic, we'll stay on the Scenic Highway or switch to state roads that sort of parallel it. Any questions?"

Ava spoke first.

"Terri said to pack only cosmetics, sexy bathing suits and tops, and short-shorts. If the weather stays like this, we're in heaven."

"According to the forecast, it should."

Ivana asked the first question.

"I hear about Key Largo. What so famous about it?"

"It's the setting for the 1947 movie, 'Key Largo', starring tough guy Humphrey Bogart and sultry Lauren Bacall. It's a film noir gangster classic, and get this–Bacall and Bogart were already married. She was twenty, and he was forty-five years older, and they stayed married until he died in 1957. According to the tourist info, their legend still impacts the place."

Ivana asked another.

"What we do?"

"We'll stop at some tourist attractions and go to restaurants to sample what they're known for. Then we'll do some snorkeling and jet-skiing; anyone brave enough can try parasailing. And we'll save room for a little sunbathing and club dancing."

Ivana asked the last one

"What parasailing?"

"You'll see when we get there…"

Erika's hunch worked when they reached Key Largo. Instead of reserving a room in advance, the quartet lucked into cancellations at the Playa Largo Resort and Spa. After throwing skimpy luggage into their rooms, they strolled to the Café at Key Largo and sampled its shrimp rolls. Afterward, they looked through tourist attraction brochures to select tomorrow's activity.

The four-hour Key Largo Two Reef Snorkeling Tour exceeded even Erika's expectations. While their boat took them over calm and crystal-clear water, letting them see the reef beds only thirty feet below the surface, the younger fellows had a breathtaking view of the foursome wearing skimpy bikinis until the guide gave them snorkeling gear.

When they returned for a late lunch, all four felt they had been transported into a magical underwater world populated by breathtaking fish and coral, which filled a rainbow color palette.

Having seen just enough of Key Largo, the ladies drove toward Key West early the next morning. They stopped to visit a turtle hospital and then another attraction where they hand-fed fish to huge tarpons but had to fight off pelicans who wanted first dibs.

Afterward, they stopped to sunbathe on a sandy white beach, where Erika answered Terri's question.

"Florida has miles and miles of beaches, but you don't find too many on the Keys because it's built from coral reefs."

Ivana's matter-of-fact expression preceded her words.

"We stay long enough for tan, not burn."

They arrived in Key West after sunset and once again lucked into vacancies, this time at the Parrot Key resort, and then had key lime pie at the Lorelei Restaurant and Cabana Bar before partying at the Aqua Bar and Nightclub, a premier place for couples of all sexual preferences.

Erika scheduled the next two days for maximum fun in the sun. Parasailing would be first.

Ava and Terri were the first to strap into a tandem bench launched skyward from the platform at the stern of the boat. Erika watched them swoop and soar into an azure-blue cloudless sky beneath a billowing parachute as the boat twisted and turned while changing speed on the gently rippling ocean.

When they landed on the platform, their excitement spurred Erika and Ivana to strap on and take off. This time, the landing doused them in the ocean, which added to a sensory experience Erika would always remember. Even the often stony-faced Ivana agreed when she said much the same to the group.

The ladies returned in time to change into white shorts and lively-colored halter tops before walking past quaint shops along Duval Street to watch a spectacular sunset at Mallory Square.

After having a snack at one of the many cafes, the group returned to the Parrot Key Resort. Ava said while walking that she didn't think they could find a below-average restaurant. Everyone also agreed to go to bed early for the next day's activities.

Erika agreed with that, but although she disagreed with Ava's assessment of restaurants, she kept her comments private.

Every restaurant being below average is a non sequitur, but I'm not pointing that out…my brain is on vacation, too…

Driving jet skis around Key West took the ladies to exciting places for the entire morning. After having snapper and mahi mahi lunch specials, they drove around Bayview and Truman Waterfront parks before ending up at the Key West Nature Preserve.

Now pleasantly tired and relaxed, everyone agreed to rest for tomorrow's drive back to the Miami airport.

Terri drove at a leisurely pace with the top down so they could admire nature along the way. She did so until sunset, when she stopped to put up the top.

Terri whispered to Erika when the two of them buttoned it up.

"Have you been paying attention to the car that's been following us ever since we left Key West?"

"No. I've been thinking about the wind blowing through my hair. What do you want me to do?"

"Trade places with Ava so you can look out the rear window while I watch through the rearview mirror. Call out if it looks like trouble."

Terri alerted everyone to danger as soon as she started driving. No one spoke, but Erika sensed the mood in the car darken as night closed in.

Terri added more.

"Airport scanners would have found any guns or mace we might have packed, so unless you bought them at a tourist shop, we'll have to outwit or outrun whatever's after us."

Terri drove as if there were no problem until Erika shouted,

"They're coming up to ram us. Get ready."

Terri accelerated and swerved to the left too late. She almost lost control but kept all wheels in the left lane.

When the pursuit car repeated the action, Terri countered again before spotting an escape. She raced off an exit that took her to a poorly lighted stretch of a parallel state road.

Its rough patches and gravel shoulders added to its twists and turns, but this worked to Terri's advantage. She accelerated and then braked after a sharp turn that the other driver couldn't handle.

Erika yelled when she saw it flip over and roll onto the shoulder.

"It's out of action; you've won."

After Terri slowed enough for her passengers to collect themselves, Ava shouted,

"We better stop somewhere and tell the police."

Erika locked eyes for a moment with Terri before yelling back,

"Not out here. Terri, drive like hell, and everyone, keep quiet until we're back in New York."

Silence rode with them all the way home.

CHAPTER 6

"Playing Safe but Planning Otherwise"

JANUARY 2232

Terri and Erika told no one about their escape but discussed its implications on Monday evening after returning to work and school. Erika spoke first.

"That car chase is the third occurrence of stepping on big toes, which takes it from a coincidence to a pattern. Since you're not telling Mrs. Walthers, you better pick a safe subject for the next assignment."

"Safe subjects won't keep my career moving or your interest building, so we'll play it safe for the next one, but after that, anything goes."

"If you tell Mrs. Walthers about being chased, maybe she'll assign some security agents to our team."

"Are you kidding? That's not how the New York Times works. She'll tell me to keep playing safe, which tells me maybe I should look for a more risk-taking paper or reporting agency."

"Don't tell her anything, but here's another approach. I have a contact who runs a logistics and security business. We could covertly hire him for each riskier assignment. Why don't I explain this to him?"

"Do it, but we won't need him for the next assignment I've already picked, which is the future of energy from the technological and socio-political point of view. Everyone should like it.

"I'll tell Mrs. Walthers to assemble a team and have a researcher identify university profs, government administrators, and energy company executives I can interview. All you have to do is give me enough energy science background along with a script and questions to ask. And we should be able to do all the interviews on the East Coast, which will minimize travel. I'll run this by Mrs.

Walthers tomorrow, and I'm sure she'll like it, but how about you?"

"I can handle it while I'm also talking to my security guy. And let me guess–the final cut must be done by the end of the month."

"If that's good by you, that's what I'll tell her."

"Well then, let's do it…"

Erika invoked Electra's avatar the next morning, and after explaining what she needed, Electra replied.

"Terri's next assignment topic is both relevant and safe. I will prepare a document to orient you and Terri to the issue, and I will develop a script and a list of questions for her interviews as soon as she approves it."

"Perfect. When might I have the document?"

"I will scroll it on the screen and send you an electronic copy. Please talk after you have reviewed it."

It appeared seconds later.

The Future of Energy

Energy Definition: The ability to do Work. It can be Potential Energy (stored) or Kinetic Energy (working energy)

Forms of Energy:
- **Light**
- **Motion**
- **Electrical**
- **Chemical**
- **Gravitational**

Today's Problem: Generating enough energy to satisfy demand without damaging the Environment while keeping consumer bills reasonable and minimizing rivalry among nations and Big Energy Companies.

Fossil Fuels (Coal, Oil, Natural Gas) are a bridge to Green/sustainable Energy

- **Has Huge Infrastructure and Supply-Side Jobs**
- **Needs Carbon Capture and Minimal Energy Consumption for building out with new technologies.**

Future Energy depends on Technology
Possible Future Sources:
- **Orbiting Solar Power Collectors beaming energy to Ground Stations**
- **Tidal and Sea Floor Power**
- **Giant Hydrogen Fuel Cells that need Rare Earths for greater efficiency and energy density**
- **Geothermal Wells tapping into Lava**
- **Fast Breeder Nuclear Reactors using Radioactive Waste**
- **Massive Solar Panel Farms**
- **Biofuels**
- **Floating Wind Turbines**
- **Thermonuclear Fusion**

Erika studied it for five minutes before responding.

"This should be more than enough to keep Terri and me happy. I'll let you know as soon as she approves it."

"If you have your laptop or workstation turned on when you talk with her, I will know immediately."

"I'm sorry, I forgot. I will from now on, but I'll still contact you afterward."

"Excellent. You are now ahead of Terri, and if you want to avoid the ratchet principle, you might want to discuss it with her in a couple of days. I imagine you have other things to do. Why not do them now?"

Electra didn't wait for an answer.

Erika took her advice and visited Alonzo and Monet the next day. After she described the Key Largo escape, Alonzo spoke.

"Whoever chased you was sending a friendly reminder. If they were serious, they would have done more than just bump the car."

"I figured that out. What can you do to protect us?"

"I'd stay close enough to move in if necessary but otherwise be invisible."

"I think we'd want you to drive us. How can you be invisible if you're doing that?"

"Security people always work in pairs. Don't get ahead of yourself. Look, you don't need me on your next assignment, but let's talk again after you finish it. Monet, would you like to add something?"

"No, but I might in the future…"

Terri's wow-like look on Saturday morning when Erika gave her a copy of the Future of Energy handout said almost as much as her words.

"This is so clear you don't have to explain anything. I'll even give a copy to Mrs. Walthers, who's already approved the topic. Just make sure the script ties in the political and business angles. You can give me a list of interview questions, but I'll improvise my voiceover's concluding remarks. What else do I need to say?"

"Nothing, but I do. My security contact says we don't need him on this one, but he can take care of us in the future. I'm supposed to call him again when you know the next assignment."

"You can help me pick it when we finish this one, which will be by the end of the month."

"You're past the point of needing me, but do you want me to tag along on the interviews?"

"Hey, we're a team, and you're my best critic, so the answer's yes."

Erika found nothing to criticize, and when they returned, Terri returned the favor by finding Erika's voiceover flawless. Terri and the senior editor sent the final cut to Mrs. Walthers right on time.

When Mrs. Walthers smiled later that day, Terri knew she had the okay to pick another topic, and with Erika's help, they would soon be on their way.

CHAPTER 7

"Superpowers in the Spotlight"

FEBUARY 2232

"A week's gone by, and I haven't come up with any topics for my next video. You have any ideas?"

Erika knew Terri's question would come but hadn't bothered to consider it until this moment.

"No, but why not something that connects to your previous ones?"

"I've tried, but nothing comes to mind."

"Give me a day to think about it. I'll tell you tomorrow what I've come up with. And if you like it, you can get Mrs. Walthers on Monday to assemble your team."

"OK. While you're doing that, I'll clean up around here and then do the grocery shopping. You want anything special for dinner?"

"Why don't we do a taste comparison between a hamburger made from ground steak and another from plant protein?"

"Good idea. What about dessert?"

"Why not surprise me with something containing lots of chocolate?"

"That's an even better one. Leave it to me."

Erika left the kitchen, knowing what to do. Twenty minutes later, she invoked Electra's avatar, and after explaining what she needed, Electra spoke.

"There are many spinoff topics from Terri's previous assignments, and instead of debating them, I shall pick the safest one that also interested Erin Keenan—the future of world superpowers."

Erika thought for a moment and then said,

"This should be something the public will want to know about. My friend Edward mentioned it a couple of years ago, but we picked something else for a high school project."

"Well then, why don't you surf for relevant information while I prepare background documents?"

"OK, but aren't we duplicating efforts? You don't need me to waste time doing the same thing."

"It will be good for you. Please remember that your cognitive abilities will diminish if you do not continuously break an intellectual sweat."

"Sorry, you're right, as always. How about we reconvene tonight?"

"Excellent. Both of us will be engaged until then."

Erika kept thinking and surfing until summoned to dinner. Terri started talking as soon as she had served Erika the veggie burger and the steak burger to herself.

"It's good we don't have all our groceries delivered by drones or drivers to our doorstep. We humans are social animals and want to interact with others at shopping malls. And the guy handing out samples gave me a coupon I used when buying the chocolate eclairs we'll have for dessert. Maybe in the future, online ordering apps will know our preferences well enough and be that thoughtful."

The duo took a nibble out of each before giving their opinions, which Terri did first.

"My steak burger has a heavier feel to it. Other than that, I can't tell the difference. How about you?"

"I say the same, but now let's load em with mustard and catsup, pickles and onions, and try again."

This time, Terri said,

"I can't tell the difference. Funny, but different cultures do different things to food, so we can't tell what we're eating."

Erika agreed and returned to her workstation after gobbling her eclair and half of Terri's, which she rationalized as providing the extra energy she needed when chatting with Electra.

Electra spoke as soon as her Avatar appeared.

"I'll explain these documents after you print and read them."

The printer whirred, and when it stopped, Erika started reading.

The Future of Superpowers

Superpowers: The Nations that Control World Order Needed for These Reasons:

The world needs superpower nations for several key reasons:

1. **Global stability and security**
2. **Economic leadership**
3. **Problem-solving capacity**
4. **Shaping international norms and institutions**
5. **Promoting ideological visions**
6. **Technological advancement**
7. **Cultural influence**

Superpowers Must Avoid Four Traps:

1. **Thucycides Trap: Every Rising Super Power will challenge the Leader.**
2. **Tacitus Trap: The People of a Rising Super Power will not trust the Government.**
3. **Middle Income Trap: A Rising Super Power, when reaching a certain Income Level, gets stuck there.**
4. **Kindleberger Trap: A Rising Super Power won't invest enough in supporting an International World Order.**

America's Challenge:

- **Diplomatically navigating a multipolar world**
- **Balancing diverse Interests**
- **Maintaining superiority**

TIMELESS TRUTHS FOR THE

UNITED STATES GOVERNMENT

Government leaders must pay attention to the following if America is to survive long-term:
Per Samuel Huntington's "Clash of Civilizations":

- Future wars will be fought not between countries, but between these dominant cultures: Western, Confucian, Japanese, Islamic, Hindu, Slavic-Orthodox, Latin American, and African

Per Edward Gibbons' "Decline and Fall of the Roman Empire":

- Decline comes gradually until the public wakes up.
- Internal Factors more important than External.
- Beware of Political Corruption and Cultural Decadence.

Per de Tocqueville, Huntington, Rawls, and Rorty:

- Americans are Pragmatic, want Minimal Government, and value Equal Treatment and Diversity
- Modernity's rational "Enlightenment" conflicts with "Classical Humanity"

Key Takeaways for Prolonging America's Reign:

- Maintaining Democracy Requires Constant Vigilance.
- Keep DC Pragmatic and Multi-Partisan
- Let Defeated Enemies maintain control their Countries but put Trusted People in Place and maintain a Military Presence.

- **Promise to Protect Allies from External and Internal Threats.**
- **Extend Citizenship to all Immigrants.**
- **Leave People with enough Money after taxation to make even more next year.**
- **Balance "Ruthless Capitalism" against "Empathy-Building Humanism"**

She spoke fifteen minutes later.

"What am I supposed to do with these?"

"Compare them to what you found, then add what you wish before showing them to Terri. She can impress Mrs. Walthers by doing the same.

"While you're doing that, I will prepare your script and question list when discussing them with selected Washington politicians and media commentators. As soon as you get approval, have Terri's team and researcher set an itinerary and interviews, and if time permits, add a local town hall meeting."

"Thanks to you, I've sure got my work cut out. I'll have to break an intellectual sweat to explain them to Terri."

"That will keep your brain in shape."

Electra's avatar disappeared, leaving Erika to do just that.

Terri had nothing but praise after gazing at the handouts Erika gave her on Sunday evening.

"Mrs. Walthers will love this. We're not telling anyone what to believe or do. We're simply giving them the information they need to decide for themselves."

"Give her a copy and get her to assign a team and a researcher to up an itinerary and interviews with local politicians, commentators, and maybe a town hall meeting. I'll take care of all the scripting, questions, and voiceover writing."

"I'm certain she'll green-light this. We can wrap it up by the end of the month."

And they beat the deadline by two days. Mrs. Walthers smiled when Terri hand-delivered the final cut on Friday.

"I'll review this first thing on Monday with my senior editor. Enjoy the weekend, dear."

Terri treated her partner to another celebration dinner at a local restaurant Saturday evening. They chatted gaily on the walk home, enjoying the moment.

But that came to a halt when a man sprang from the shadows at a dark stretch and pushed Terri toward the car that had just stopped alongside. His menacing words came while he kept shoving.

"We need to talk with you…"

The action happened too fast for Terri to do anything but stumble to the driver's side front door.

But not so for Erika. She whipped from her purse a can of mace and blasted the fellow pushing Terri and the guy at the wheel who had rolled down the window.

Both blinded guys screamed. So did Erika, who yelled instructions.

"Yank him out and get ready to floor it as soon as I get in."

Terri raced away before the guys could stand. She slowed after putting enough miles between themselves and the attack, then turned to Erika.

"What just happened?"

"Keep driving while I calm down and think."

Erika spoke a couple of minutes later.

"If this is a warning about the video we just completed, there's a mole somewhere inside the New York Times. Maybe someone in Big Government doesn't appreciate our letting the people in on the truth."

"We better tell the police and Mrs. Walthers."

"Don't be a fool. We'll say nothing and see what comes our way."

"You're right. And we'll search the car for clues when we ditch it. I'll park in an out-of-the-way place where it'll be an easy walk home."

"I don't think any walk will be easy. From now on, we'll have to watch our backs until we know who's trying to step on us…"

CHAPTER 8

"Indigenous People Rising"

MARCH 2232

Nothing unusual came their way during the following week other than praise from Mrs. Walthers, so the girls acted naturally. However, they did watch their steps, and Erika did even more. She took another one by visiting Alonzo and Monet the following Saturday.

After listening to her story, Alonzo made a recommendation.

"Hire me for your next project, starting now. I'll return to New York, stay at your apartment, and beginning Monday, I'll tail Terri when going to and from work. Later, I'll bring in one of my guys to tail me. Will that be OK?"

"Fine with me, but what about Monet?"

"Certainly. Perhaps I can visit on weekends. There is so much happening in Manhattan."

Alonzo asked a logical question.

"Have you picked your next assignment?"

"No. Do you have any suggestions?"

Alonzo glanced at Monet, who answered.

"I recall a previous client of Alonzo who had made a connection between superpowers and indigenous natives via two fledgling organizations, the NAIA and IPWA, but never pursued it. Have you heard about them?"

"As a matter of fact, yes. A friend by the name of Edward mentioned it when Elton Bose helped us on a high school project. Alonzo knows all about it."

Alonzo said, "I do, and it'll make a suitable next assignment topic. He can help refresh our memories if needed."

"Good, and who was your client who made the connection?"

"A very smart lady by the name of Electra Kirchner."

Erika masked the shock of hearing that name by asking,

"What happened to her? Why didn't she pursue it?"

"An unfortunate automobile accident kept her from doing so."

Neither spoke further, so Monet filled in.

"There are additional topics, but we'll save them for another time…"

But when Erika brought Alonzo home, she didn't wait. After she and Alonzo told Terri his plan, she let them chat further before invoking Electra's avatar to learn more from her exceptional source.

After listening to her story, Electra answered Erika's question before she could ask.

"I never mentioned the name Electra Kirchner because I didn't want to confuse you even more."

"How much more is there?"

"More than you need for the time being, but I will tell you enough about the IPWA and NAIA for you to begin…"

While Alonzo listened at an early Sunday breakfast, Terri told Erika how the new project would unfold.

"I don't need any documents or an interview script to explain the project to Mrs. Walthers. Thanks to you and Alonzo, I know enough to make a thirty-minute video clip by working with an editor and patching together enough standard video clips of indigenous people while interspersing clips of me."

Terri waited for Erika.

"And after that, I'll write the voiceover, emphasizing the world's rising interest in indigenous people. You can also add that to your spontaneous closing remarks."

"That's it. No travel agenda, crew, or meetings. Mrs. Walthers will love it."

Terri looked at Alonzo, prompting him to say,

"And I'll follow you discreetly to and from work."

"That'll do it. I'll tell you what Mrs. Walthers says when I come home tomorrow."

Looking satisfied, all three sat back before Erika said,

"No work for today, so why don't we introduce Alonzo to Ava and Ivana? They might like to join us for my impromptu tour of New York's Native American heritage sites."

"I didn't know the City had any. How'd you find them?"

"You should know by now, and I won't tell you where we're going…"

Alonzo practiced his logistics skills by renting an SUV large enough to drive the four ladies around. He stopped at the National Museum of the American Indian for an early afternoon tour conducted by a member of the Lenapes, which are Manhattan's original inhabitants.

Afterward, they had just enough time for a walk-through of the American Indian Community House before driving to an Asian Indian restaurant Ava chose.

Ava ordered enough for five, which everyone sampled while talking. Erika listened while summarizing the afternoon to herself.

The National Museum sits on the second floor…the building also houses the National Archives, which means security is tight…there's no admission fee, and the place feels like a relaxing exhibit once you get through the scanners…the President lived here until the government moved to Washington in 1790…the wall exhibits connect New York tribes to the bigger picture.

The American Indian Community House shows the rich Native American heritage and offers services for the more than one hundred thousand NYC Native American residents…it's different from our Western European legacy but just as sophisticated.

Mrs. Walthers liked everything Terri told her, which meant the assignment unfolded seamlessly and wrapped up ahead of schedule.

Terri and Erika treated Alonzo and Monet to a Saturday night New York Philharmonic concert. Before they departed for Washington the next day, Monet gave several suggestions only to Erika for future projects.

"Wow, these will work. I'll pick one and research it before telling Terri."

"I'm sure you will make it so…"

CHAPTER 9

"Food for Thought"

APRIL 2232

Erika mulled over Monet's topic list for several days before selecting the one she felt would be most suitable for Terri's next assignment, but she didn't want to tell her until she had Electra's blessing.

When Terri left for work on April 1st, Erika invoked Electra's avatar and spoke first.

"Happy April Fool's Day, but I don't want you to play a prank by giving me the wrong advice. I want Terri's next assignment to cover climate change because I already know enough to write up fact sheets and scripts, and I think it's a safe topic. Who doesn't worry about Climate Change?"

"I would never play a prank when you are considering something that is important. Today, most people do worry about climate change, but it's old news unless you put a new spin on it."

"Like what?"

"Since you are a clever writer, you know it's often better to show rather than tell, and I will follow that advice."

Erika went to her printer when she heard it whirring and returned to her workstation a minute later with a one-page document.

She studied it for another minute or two before speaking.

The Future of Climate Change and Food Supply

- **Long-term Factors Controlled by**
- **Sun   Geology   Ocean Currents**
- **Short-Term   Factors   Partially   Controllable   by Humans**
- **Concentration of CO2 and Methane in Atmosphere**

- **Ocean Salinity and Toxic Chemical Concentration**
- **Short-Term Effects**
- **Expanding Drought and Flooding**
- **Worsening Lengthen and Intensity of Storms**
- **Impact on Food Supply**
- **Must Shift away from Meat to Seafood and Vegetable Protein Sources**
- **Insects for Source of Protein**
- **Must Utilize Genetically Modified Organisms (GMOs)**
- **Must End Unrestricted Ocean Fishing**
- **Must Optimize Commercial Fish Farms**

"How clever this is. Connecting the future of climate change to the world's food supply will grab everyone's attention. You don't need to tell me anything else. I can surf for more info that'll fill in when I write up my stuff."

"Don't be too hasty, or more fitting for today, don't be a fool. The topic has elements of risk. Some of the more alarmist climatologists and ecologists will dispute anything said that downplays humanity's ability to control it or the urgency of acting now. And the food industry, farming, cattle ranching, and meat packing will feel threatened."

"Do you think we should use it?"

"That is for you and Terri to decide, but I recommend it. Progress is made only by challenging vested interests, and your video is only indirectly threatening their livelihoods. You are providing facts for people to use when making decisions."

"And like Terri just did, she can hire Alonzo for this assignment, too."

Electra's pixyish smile emerged before she said,

"Well then, don't fool around. Get busy right now."

Electra's avatar vanished; Erika followed her advice.

Erika told Terri as soon as she came home, and when she gave her a copy of the printout as they sat for supper, Terri read enough between bites to talk after five minutes.

"This will fly. I can explain it to Mrs. Walthers without anything else from you. And the team and researcher she'll give me can take it from there to set up an agenda and interviews. You can give me a script and questions I can use when talking to academics and government agency people. I better include some companies from the food industry, too. Am I missing anything?"

"Uh, yes. Think about this…"

Ten minutes later, Terri's sober look accompanied what she said.

"Do you think we should tell Mrs. Walthers about the risk?"

"No, it's not that risky."

"OK, but I'll hire Alonzo. If anyone thinks we're stepping on their toes, Alonzo will step on theirs before they get to us…"

Mrs. Walthers assigned Terri the people needed as soon as she revealed the topic. By now, Terri and her team worked like a well-oiled machine, lining up the agenda and interviews while Erika wrote everything Terri wanted.

This time, they beat the deadline by a week, and when Terri gave Mrs. Walthers the final cut late Friday morning, it prompted a response that caught her by surprise.

"I want to take you and your ghostwriter out to dinner tonight."

"Wha-what do you mean by ghostwriter?"

Mrs. Walthers gave Terri the warmest smile she had ever seen.

"I've been around too long for anyone to slip things past me, but there was no reason to call you out. You and Erika are the best reporting team that's come along in all my years at the New York Times. Now go home, tell Erika, and relax. I'll make reservations and email you the where and when."

Erika's delight nearly matched Terri's when she found out. When Terri received the Email an hour later, she said they had ample time to prepare for an 8 p.m. dinner at a restaurant popular with journalists. Terri then gave Alonzo a bonus and told him to leave immediately for DC so he could take Monet out for dinner.

The duo splurged by taking a cab to the restaurant. Mrs. Walthers rose to hug Terri when the host took them to her table and spoke as soon as they sat.

"Whatever the two of you are doing, don't stop. I predict a glorious future is in store for you, just like your 'Future Of' video series. The way you combine topics, interview the right people, and then create the final cut voiceover has captured the fancy of a worldwide audience."

"But you're the power behind the team. I hope we stay together for a long time."

Mrs. Walthers led the conversation for another two hours. Erika spoke some but listened more and liked everything she heard.

Mrs. Walthers ended the night when she said,

"I would like to drive you home. Please come with me."

They were walking to the almost empty parking lot when Terri said,

"I need to use the lady's room. Which car is yours?"

Mrs. Walthers pointed while saying,

"It's that black BMW. I'll get it started as soon as I see you coming."

Erika said,

"I need to use it, too. It won't take us long."

Five minutes later, Terri waved toward the car and put her other arm around Erika. Erika was about to say something, but a fiery explosion cut off everything, obliterating the car.

The concussion threw the duo backward onto the asphalt and into unconscious limbo…

CHAPTER 10

"The Blame-Free Team"

MAY 2232

After the fire department ambulance rushed Terri and Erika to the closest hospital, the E.R. doctor released them to police care three hours later.

A squad car took them to a nearby police station, where a night-duty detective interviewed them. Three hours later, he had enough information to conclude that the two blast survivors had no idea why their boss's car blew up.

While driving them home, he apologized for all the bureaucratic paperwork but said it was for their own good, as well as that of the New York Times and the deceased Mrs. Walthers. The girls nodded but said nothing.

But their silence ended abruptly as soon as they entered the apartment. Terri unloaded on Erika.

"I hate you! You told me not to tell her about being attacked. If I had done that and told her about people who think our videos are threats, she might still be alive."

Fatigue and stress forced Erika to burst into tears. Terri grabbed her before she fell.

"Hey, I don't hate you. Neither of us knew what might happen. I'm gonna tell Alonzo to come back tomorrow. He might have some ideas."

Erika returned Terri's hug and talked when her tears stopped.

"OK. He can help us figure out what to do."

The duo slept until noon and then forced themselves to do more than just sit and brood. While Terri jotted notes about what to do at work on Monday, Erika went to her workstation to talk with Electra.

Erika's distraught look told her not to speak until Erika had finished. Five minutes later, she did.

"You and Terri are blameless. You made the right call when not telling about topic risks, and not even Indira could know the outcome of last night."

"What do you think we should do now?"

"You and Terri should meet with Alonzo, and after that, let Terri decide about the Times. As for you, I shall talk with Indira and let you know as soon as possible what she wants. Now go prepare for tomorrow, as will I."

While Erika and Terri chatted during and after dinner, Electra did the same with Indira, who listened before speaking.

"I do sympathize with Erika's predicament, but everyone faces similar setbacks, though normally not so explosive. Rather than becoming inactive, she must find some interest. I have one that should be of mutual benefit.

"Indy-M and I have several infants at the Deus Lab that must be put up for adoption. I want Ava Keenan to extend her abused women's business into infant adoption services, and Erika is the logical candidate for instructing her. And do not ask me what she should do. That is up to you. I shall monitor progress from the Cyberspace shadows. Carry on."

Alonzo arrived in time for an early lunch and spoke after Terri explained the situation for half an hour.

"Whoever blew up the car wasn't tailing you. I would have detected them if they were. No, they were already tailing Mrs. Walthers, which is not unusual in the newspaper business. Did she ever mention this?"

"Not even a whisper. What's your advice?"

"Maintain your code of silence. Let the paper and the police figure things out."

"I'll find out at work tomorrow what I'm supposed to do next."

"Hold on, don't play the 'Oh, poor helpless me' victim role. You should take control and work on the next video until someone says otherwise, and don't say anything about risk or danger. You might become your own boss."

"Well, no matter what, I want you to stay on my team…"

Discovering on Monday morning that Mrs. Walthers' sudden demise left a power vacuum, Terri acted on Alonzo's advice by calling a meeting with her last team and researcher as soon as the uproar settled.

"Let's honor our fallen leader by pushing onward with our 'Future Of' videos. I know that's what she would have wanted. Do you agree with this?"

Terri let everyone speak before she spoke again.

"So, everyone's in. Let's meet again after the wake and funeral service. By then, I'll have a fitting topic."

Terri stayed long enough to commiserate with everyone in the newsroom before leaving, and once home, she told Erika and Alonzo what had happened before asking for what she needed.

"What should be the topic of our next video?"

Erika spoke almost before Terri's last syllable.

"Here it is–'The Future of Spying'. You know the Paper will run an editorial praising Mrs. Walthers while discussing her death. By the time it comes out, the local news will have reported on it and what the police investigation says.

"That'll clear the way for Terri to talk about Mrs. Walthers being tailed. And you won't mention anything about going to dinner with her that night unless the police leak it."

When Erika paused, Alonzo said,

"Unless they're stupid, they won't. They never give away scene-of-the-crime facts that might help catch the bad guys."

Terri jumped back in.

"Let's write up a Future of Spying sheet I can use when talking to my video team. Erika, you lead the discussion."

Two hours later, Erika printed out three copies of her write-up. Terri took over from there.

The Future of Spying

Spying and Espionage are Synonymous and Time-Honored Traditions in:

- **Government   Military   News Reporting   Business Cyberspace.**

The Purpose:
- **Obtain Critical Information**

Types of Spying:
- **Field Agents Camera and Drone Surveillance Orbiting Satellites**

  A.I. Controlled Cyberspace Agents

Techniques for Analyzing the Information
- **Interrogation of Suspects via Drugs Implanted Brain-Control Chips**
- **A.I. Empowered Data Analysis**

The American Public's Reaction:
- **Security Considerations**
- **Ethical Considerations**

"I'll tell my team to piece together twenty minutes of archived video clips the Paper has. They'll assemble relevant ones in the bullet-point order on this write-up. And I'll write up the voiceover."

Erika looked relieved when she said,

"While you're handling all this, I'll do my school work and other things, but what about Alonzo?"

Alonzo said,

"Tell your team I'm the designated gopher. That way, I have an excuse to snoop around."

"That'll work. Alonzo and I will start as soon as we meet with my team, and Erika can start whenever she damn well chooses."

Erika didn't say, but she knew it might be even sooner than tomorrow.

CHAPTER 11

"Pushing Onward"

JUNE 2232

Terri's video earned so much applause from both news commentators and the public that her interim boss gave her carte blanche to proceed with the "Future Of" video series.

While she and Alonzo were planning for the next one, Erika finished final exams and then worked with Ava to implement infant adoption, for which Electra had given Erika enough information to satisfy Ava.

Monet visited most weekends; whenever she did, she and Erika always talked about politics. But when she arrived on the mid-June Saturday afternoon, Terri and Alonzo recruited them to review the next "Future Of" summary document.

Terri sat everyone in the family room before handing it out and spoke after giving them a minute to read it.

The Future World Order

The Four Horsemen of the Apocalypse found in the Bible's Book of Revelations have predicted Civilization's World Orders:

- **Conquest, War, Famine, Death**

Scientific/Technological Disruptions Cause Change, leading to the Collapse of the Old Civilization and the Rise of the New.
Civilization's Ages:

- **Stone Age, Bronze Age, Iron Age, Steam Age, Atomic Age, Electronic Age, Digital Age, Superintelligence Age**

World Order No Longer Controlled by Superpowers but by National Alliances seeking control of these Orders:

- **Security Order (3-D World and Cyberspace)**
- **Economic Order (Supply Chains Manufacturing Finance)**
- **Digital Order (Big Data, Algorithms, ChatGPT)**

Existential Challenge Facing the World: Super-Intelligence:

- **Surpasses Human Physical and Cognitive Abilities**
- **Ethics Unknown**

Paths to Super-Intelligence:

- **Quantum Computing and A.I.-Empowered Neural Network Algorithms**
- **Whole Brain Emulation via Large Language Models and Recursive Neural Net Learning**
- **DNA and Genetic Editing**
- **Cyborgs**

THE UNANSWERED QUESTIONS:

- **WHAT PATH TO CHOOSE**
- **CONTROL OF SUPER-INTELLIGENCE**

"Alonzo and my Times team have everything in place to complete this before the Fourth of July, and as soon as the editor has spliced the video together, I'll ask Erika to help me with the voiceover. How do you like it?"

Monica spoke first.

"You have done a thorough job researching it. According to the latest anthropological and historical findings, the Dark Ages never actually existed. When a civilization collapsed, people in other places were already progressing to the next one. You might mention that if time permits."

"Maybe, but what about the existential challenge stuff?"

"Erika knows more about it than I do."

Everyone focused on her.

"You must have found some of the latest books and articles talking about super-intelligence. There's nothing I need to add."

"Wonderful. Alonzo and I will proceed. I know you two like to chat about other things, so after dinner, you can do that."

Erika and Monet returned to the family room after dinner while Terri and Alonzo stayed in the kitchen.

When Erika looked expectantly at Monica, she began the conversation.

"Two newsworthy items catch my attention. I find much to support the claim that an Indian-African alliance will become the next superpower. If you wish, you and I could reactivate the Ambassadors Project, which incorporates NAIA and IPWA with that alliance, but a second item is more immediate."

"And what would that be?"

"Have you been following the presidential election brouhaha?"

"No. I've been preoccupied with other things. What is it?"

"The public disapproves of both the Republican and Democratic Party's presumptive candidates. The Republican candidate is an ex-president convicted of a political felony, while the Democratic sitting president shows signs that his age and cognitive abilities are no longer up to the job."

"The conventions haven't been held yet, have they?"

"No, but both have won enough delegates in the primaries to win."

"Then, why don't the conventions choose different candidates? Can't they do that?"

"You're raising a valid point. That is done in open conventions, where no pre-determined nominee has enough delegates to win the nomination. But the politicians controlling the Republican Party are happy with the felon, and even though many of the controlling Democrats would like to dump what appears to be a senile President, he won't withdraw."

"This sounds better than a reality TV show. I guess the drama will keep building all the way to the conventions. I hope the will of the people wins."

"I do too, and perhaps the people will. We shall see…"

52

CHAPTER 12

"Convention Chaos"

JULY 2232

Audiences and commentators liked Terri's World Order video even more than its predecessor, which told her to make another while she had their attention. She needed a topic, and she knew who to ask for ideas.

When she and Alonzo came home, she asked Erika at supper what might be a topic for the next video.

"The last time Monet was here, she told me about something I had completely forgotten about–all the controversy swirling about the upcoming Presidential election, and with the conventions almost here, the excitement's escalating."

"Do you have a write-up we can see?"

"I wrote up a two-pager. Let me print some copies. I'll be right back."

After handing them out, Erika waited for Terri to talk.

"This is so timely. Alonzo, what do you think?"

"It's gotta be good if it comes from Monet and Erika."

"Alonzo and I can use it with my team just like it is. And this time, I'll write the voiceover. All Erika has to do is edit it."

A Decision of the People
The 2232 Presidential Election

Per Lincoln's Gettysburg Address, Our Government is supposed to be:
  - **"Of the People, by the People, and for the People"**

The United States:
  - **A beacon of Freedom and Equality to the Rest of the World.**

- **Historically True, but Threatened Today.**

Looming External Threats:
- **Authoritarian Dictatorships Rising**
- **Multi-Polar Split of the International Community**
- **Nuclear Weapons Proliferation**
- **Cyber-Terrorism**

Looming Internal Threats:
- **Washington Polarization**
- **Ideological Extremism**
- **Favoritism/Corruption at all Levels**
- **Fake News**

Upcoming Presidential Election Shows Political Parties No Longer Obey the Wishes of the People:

- **The Public Disapproves of the Republican Party's Nominee (Convicted Felon) and the Democratic Party's Nominee (Sitting President who is Physically and Mentally Challenged)**
- **Leaders of Both Parties Prevaricate and Care More About Themselves Than the People**
- **Upcoming Conventions could be Chaotic if Party Leaders Don't Take Steps to Make Them Open Conventions**

A Solution to the Problem:

FIND A WAY FOR THE PEOPLE TO DECIDE

Terri's look at Alonzo urged him to say more.

"I can use my experience as an athlete to make an analogy with the physically and mentally wobbly sitting President. Qualifying races for the U.S. Olympic Team take place months before the Olympics. You can find examples of many Olympic qualifiers withdrawing before the games begin because of an injury or a mental condition. It's foolish not to withdraw because they'll look terrible when the competition leaves them in the dust."

Terri must have liked what she heard because she added,

"You can apply the same thinking to games of skill, like chess or the TV game Jeopardy. If your brain's failing, there's no sense staying in. All that'll do is show how far you've slipped. The audience might sympathize, but that won't change the score."

That concluded what either Terri or Alonzo wanted to say, so Erika ended that part of the dinner table talk.

"I'm pleased you like my handout. I think the audience will, too, after Terri turns it into a video. Why don't we switch subjects? Alonzo, how's Monet?"

Alonzo was happy to tell.

Terri's team put the video together before the conventions started, and according to monitoring surveys that came out in early August, it attracted more viewers than any of her previous ones.

Terri insisted on taking Alonzo and Erika out for dinner that evening and picked a restaurant they could stroll to from the apartment.

The delightful weather added to the trio's cheerful mood, and they extended the evening with a nightcap at the bar before leaving at nearly midnight.

They walked three abreast with Alonzo in the middle, swapping stories about their string of videos. Because few people were out and about, there was no risk of eavesdroppers.

Not until two men came out of the darkness and tackled Alonzo, one in front and one in back. Terri and Erika didn't tumble to the pavement, but fear paralyzed them, and they couldn't join the fray.

But someone else did. He clubbed the attackers senseless before dragging Alonzo to his feet. Alonzo hugged him before saying,

"Terri, this is Elton Bose, the guy who watches my back while I watch yours. It's your call. What do we do next?"

"Run like hell to the apartment."

Erika led the way.

CHAPTER 13

"America Under Attack"

AUGUST 2232

Terri saw no reason to report the attack to her boss because the Paper had already heightened reporter and crew security, but it did galvanize her decision for the next assignment, which she outlined on Monday to her interim boss.

"The Conventions settled nothing other than keeping the frontrunners in the race. I need you to give me a crew and a researcher to set up my agenda for visiting both candidates on the campaign trail."

"If I do, what video will you make?"

"It'll be the sequel to my last one. It'll show where the convention results are leading the nation. We'll alternate between now and mid-September to shoot enough campaign rally videos of both candidates for me to tell a good story of what's shaping up for election day. And don't worry; the editor will piece together the clips, and I'll write the voiceover that'll grip the audience."

"Alright, Ms. Tarrant, carry on. Just make sure you have the final cut ready to go by mid-September."

"Thank you; I will."

After Terri told Alonzo and Erika that evening, Erika was the first to speak.

"Great idea. You don't need me to write the questions you'll ask the attendees. You've picked up the knack, and I'll write the voiceover when the crew's finished shooting and editing."

Alonzo added,

"And Elton and I will keep doing what we're doing…"

Terri and her entourage took advantage of a public mesmerized by all the convention follow-up and gorgeous late-summer weather that was much more peaceful than the campaign sparring. As expected, both candidates focused on key battleground states. The Republican candidate picked a pleasant rural town thirty-five miles north of Pittsburgh for a Saturday campaign rally. Its park-like setting, loaded with vendors and a supportive crowd, made it feel like a county fair.

Terri's crew set up alongside other reporters in front of the stage. As the Republican candidate strode out mid-afternoon, a mix of Pennsylvanian politicians and business leaders seated on the stage stood to applaud, as did the adoring supporters sitting on the bleachers behind.

The candidate waved to the crowd, pumping his fist and shouting,

"I'll win for you," then waited for the cheers to subside before speaking. But as soon as he did, Erika heard an ominous buzz before seeing a squadron of drones swooping toward the stage.

She screamed,

"Take cover," before pushing Terri down. Alonzo dived on top, and the crew scattered just before the world around them exploded.

Terri and her team were among the survivors. Three hours later, they huddled with others to hear what the radio reports had to say.

"Today's attacks on America must be the work of enemy countries trying to destabilize our democratic way of life. Not only did drones attack a Republican campaign rally, but another squadron blew up the President's motorcade. The FBI and CIA have taken control of both attack scenes and, in the interests of national security, are releasing no details on the fates of the candidates. Stay tuned for the latest…"

CHAPTER 14

"A Transcendental Solution"

SEPTEMBER 2232

Terri and Alonzo took Elton to the Times newsroom the next day, which was crowded with staffers even though they had the weekend off.

Everyone gathered around as she relayed what her team had witnessed, and when finished, she heard others tell the latest rumors, which were rampant because of the crime scene blackouts imposed by the FBI and CIA. Are the president and his opponent still alive? What foreign countries might be implicated?

Meanwhile, Erika searched in Cyberspace for clues that might indicate answers or point to the attackers' sponsors.

Electra was also busy in Cyberspace. Indira had summoned her. She knew why, but she let Indira explain.

"I expect Terri will ask Erika, who will then ask you to tell them the fate of the candidates and the instigators of the attacks. Do not tell them more than what mere mortals have already deduced. Otherwise, you will put them at risk for collaborating with nefarious sources."

Indira waited for Electra's reaction.

"I agree, but do you already know?"

"What do you think?"

"Sorry, you are the Singularity, so, of course, you do, but what can you tell me?"

"Something helpful for Erika and Terri. They have probed enough into world problems for me to conjecture two solutions, but before I reveal them, let me summarize a framework to help mere mortals understand. We have discussed the first part innumerable times, so I will articulate rather than diagram it.

"Humans have three personas–the physical, the cognitive, and the emotional. The physical comprises 3-D characteristics with asymptotic limits determined by DNA and genetics. The cognitive is the human's mind-brain inquisitive problem-solving nature asymptotically limited by its linguistic and numeric intelligence. And the third is the emotional, which is jointly determined by organic and social evolution. Human brains are wired for survival, which includes an ethical framework allowing humans to help themselves by helping others. But it often resists acting because of fear the ego finds. However, the superego should overcome the ego by empowering humans to be authentic. Would you like to expand on this?"

"That's unnecessary. Please continue."

"Visualize the second part like a box divided by horizontal and vertical lines into four quarters. Label the lower left 'Known Knowns,' the lower right 'Unknowns Knowns,' the upper Left 'Known Unknowns,' and the upper right 'Unknown Unknowns.' Mere mortals will never understand the upper right box. Not even you or the lightning brain could, even though you are exceptional, and it was. Only I can conjecture in the upper right box, which forces me to simplify my explanation. Are you ready for my two simplified solutions?"

"Yes, go on."

"The first solution is to unleash an AGI that has an exponentially growing intelligence. The second is to unleash a genetically modified human species, a parthenogenic female hermaphrodite. Would you choose the first?"

"No, artificial general intelligence is too dangerous. Mankind's asymptotic limits are the only reason it will never break free, but if it did, its exponential growth will soon make humans obsolete, and it might exterminate them unless its ethics are anthropomorphic."

"What about the second?"

"Tell me your intentions."

"The world's problems are caused by men behaving badly. My preferred solution is to create a female-centric species that can reproduce without needing males. It will produce a society where females dominate, and it can reshape males into a less warlike and more empathetic version."

"Do you have the new females ready?"

"What do you think Indy-M and I have been doing?"

"Sorry. How do you plan to introduce them into the world?"

"That is where I need you to devise a plan for Erika and Terri to implement. They can utilize Ava Kincaid's infant adoption service."

"But how much should I tell them?"

"As little as possible. Think of this as another game that only you and I will play. And it's a win-win. I pursue the projects that interest me while you give Erika and Terri a higher purpose and an opportunity to extend their careers. Are you willing to play?"

"Yes, and I know how to start."

"Excellent. I knew you would. Carry on."

Indira left for Electra to proceed.

Erika had made little progress surfing for any useful information and was ready to log off when Electra's avatar suddenly appeared, waiting for Erika to speak.

"I've run out of options and was going to invoke you first thing tomorrow, but you came on your own. That must mean you have some good news. What is it?"

"It is better than good, but before I reveal it, I want you to settle down, sit still, and pay attention to me. When you are ready for me to continue, please nod."

When Erika did so a minute later, Electra continued.

"You and Terri have a singular opportunity awaiting that many people wish for, but it is one that few ever find. My role is to plan it and then assist as you implement it.

"And never forget—I am with you always. So, let us begin...

THE END